This Walker book belongs to:

For Hannah Stowe, a true ocean
wanderer, with love
N.D.

For David and Christine
S.R.

First published 2020 by Walker Books Ltd
87 Vauxhall Walk, London SE11 5HJ ● This edition published 2021
1 2 3 4 5 6 7 8 9 10 ● Text © 2020 Nicola Davies ● Illustrations © 2020
Salvatore Rubbino ● The right of Nicola Davies and Salvatore Rubbino to be
identified as author and illustrator respectively of this work has been asserted
by them in accordance with the Copyright, Designs and Patents Act 1988
This book has been typeset in Spinnaker ● Printed in China ● All rights reserved.
No part of this book may be reproduced, transmitted or stored in an infor-
mation retrieval system in any form or by any means, graphic, electronic or
mechanical, including photocopying, taping and recording, without prior
written permission from the publisher. ● British Library Cataloguing in Publication
Data: a catalogue record for this book is available from the British Library
ISBN 978-1-4063-9458-0 ● www.walker.co.uk

WALKER BOOKS
AND SUBSIDIARIES
LONDON ● BOSTON ● SYDNEY ● AUCKLAND

A NOTE FROM THE AUTHOR

Wandering albatrosses have the biggest wingspan
of any bird: up to 3.7 m.

They spend most of their lives flying over the
Southern Ocean, travelling as much as 120,000
km every year, and only return to land every two
years to join their lifelong mate and rear a single
chick. But sometimes they get caught in fishing
gear, or swallow plastic mistaking it for food, and
never make it home.

17 of the 22 different species of albatross are
threatened with extinction.

Ride the Wind

NICOLA DAVIES

illustrated by

SALVATORE RUBBINO

THE MAGDALENA pitched and rolled in the rough sea. Waves burst over her bow and flooded her decks with icy water.

Javier was exhausted, but he would not show it. Since his mother had died, his father Tomas was quick to call him weak and childish. Javier would not give him the excuse.

Seabirds crowded round the boat – gulls, petrels and albatrosses – all trying to snatch a meal from the fishing hooks. Sometimes they'd get hooked themselves. Javier hoped none would be caught today.

But when he looked up from his work, a bird
hung from the line: an albatross!

Uncle Felipe pulled the hook from its beak and flung
the bird across the deck. It landed in a heap and lay still.

"No slacking there!" Tomas shouted from the
wheelhouse. "Fish don't wait for lazy boys."

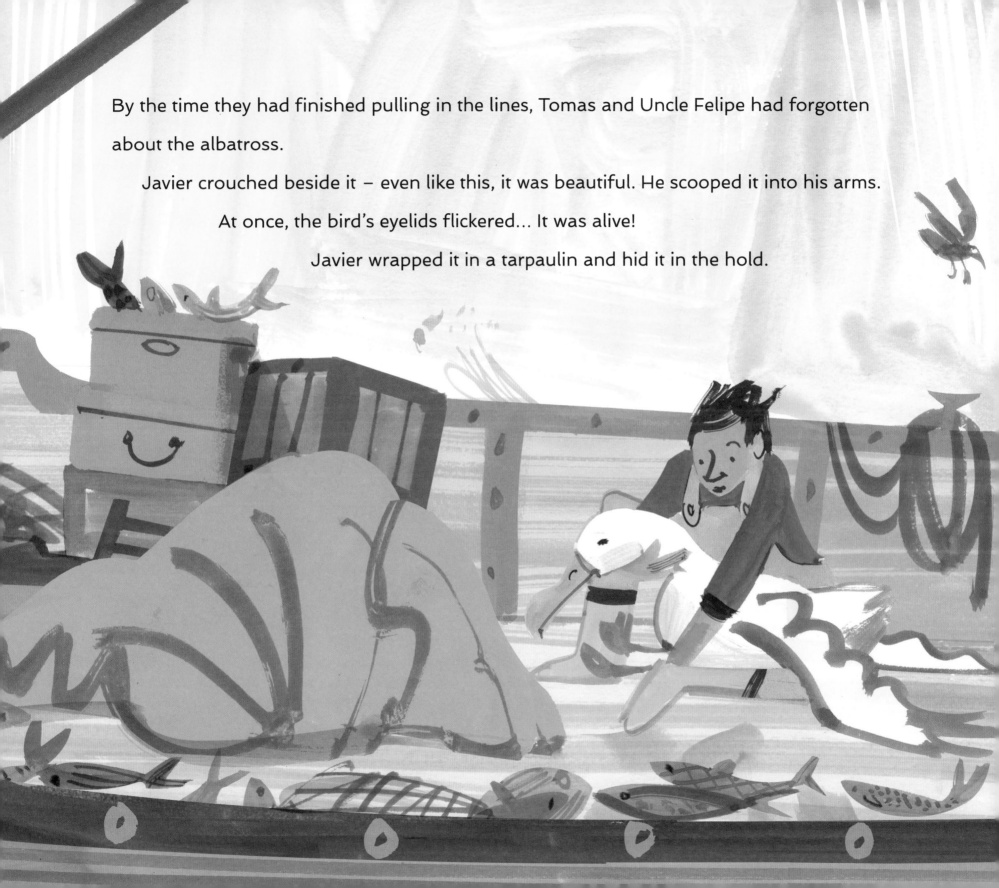

By the time they had finished pulling in the lines, Tomas and Uncle Felipe had forgotten about the albatross.

Javier crouched beside it – even like this, it was beautiful. He scooped it into his arms.

At once, the bird's eyelids flickered... It was alive!

Javier wrapped it in a tarpaulin and hid it in the hold.

The sun was high by the time they got back to the village, and the colours of the little houses gleamed against the green slopes and clifftops. The *Magdalena* chugged into port like a clucking hen – and Javier never grew tired of seeing his home from the sea like this.

When Tomas and Felipe went off to sell their catch, Javier snuck the albatross off the boat and into the storeroom behind the house. He parted the tarpaulin, afraid that the bird might have died – but a bright, brown eye stared out at him.

He put the bird in his old playpen. Once, long ago, before his mother had gone to the city to work, the playpen had kept him safe while she cooked and cleaned. His mother had never come back – but it would keep the albatross safe, all the same.

After a fishing trip, his father did little more than sleep – and Felipe went off to see his girlfriend. Javier was free to gather all he needed for the albatross...

Señora Araya gave him ointments
to heal its wounds.

Señor Ortiz let Javier have his
dog's old bed for a nest.

Señorita Vidal let him buy the smallest fish for just a little money.

Soon the bird learned that Javier brought food and clacked its beak in greeting.

Javier was sure the bird was a female.

He wondered if her mate was waiting for her somewhere, far away.

Keeping a secret in the village was impossible. When Tomas found out about the bird,
he was furious.

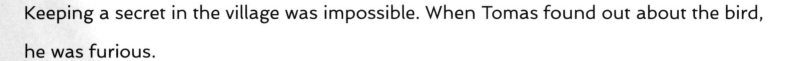

"Get that thing out of here now!" he growled.

"Please, Father, let me keep her till she can fly," Javier begged.

"Let it stay until we go to sea again," said Felipe. "What's the harm?"

Tomas scowled. "You've got two weeks until the next trip."

And he stormed out.

Uncle Felipe patted his nephew's shoulder. "Why do you care so much about the bird?"

Javier looked at the ground. "She reminds me of Mother ...

alone and sick and far from home."

Every day, the start of their next trip grew closer.

Every day the albatross ate more and more. But she showed no signs of wanting to use her wings and only shuffled her feathers like an old lady shifting her skirts.

The day before they were due to sail, Javier was frantic with worry.

"Cheer up!" Señorita Vidal told him. "There's a big wind coming! No one will be going to sea tomorrow."

Javier ran all the way home. That "big wind" had given him an idea.

But when he opened the door of the storeroom, the albatross had gone.

Javier ran to the quay – Tomas was sorting out gear on the *Magdalena*'s deck.

"What have you done with her?" Javier shouted. He had never spoken to his father like this before. "*Tell me!*"

"Sold her," said Tomas without looking up, "to Señor Tapia, who runs the fairground in Santa Crista."

"But she needs our help, like Mother did!" Javier cried. "And you *sold* her?"

He didn't wait for Tomas to reply. He just ran.

There was only one hotel in the village, newly built, out on the coast road. Señor Tapia's car was there with a big wire cage in the back.

Javier smashed his way into the car and took the bird from her prison. The police would be called, but he didn't care.

There was a wheelbarrow by the wall and he put the bird inside. Then he started to run, wheeling her up towards the clifftop where the wind was already strong.

Of course the albatross had not wanted to fly in that stuffy little room. She needed the wind to remind her who she was, and where she needed to be.

The flashing lights of police cars were winding up towards them. It was now or never: fly or die.

Javier turned the wheelbarrow into the wind and ran towards the cliff edge.

In front of the police cars, Tomas sat in Felipe's jeep – wishing it would go faster.

"I've been a fool, Felipe," he said. "I've thought only that I lost a wife, never that

Javier lost a mother."

He leapt from the car just in time to see his son running straight for the cliff edge.

It was like a nightmare. He saw the wheelbarrow tip and send boy and bird flying ...

and then, they were gone.

Javier and the bird were falling.

For a moment, their eyes met – and Javier thought of his mother.

"Go home!" he told the albatross. "Go home!"

Something in the creature's eyes answered him … and her wings snapped open.

Tomas found the boy sprawled on the very, very edge. So nearly gone!

He took his son in his arms and held him, knowing that nothing, nothing, nothing in all the world was more precious.

Javier's face was wet with tears, but lit up with a smile exactly like his mother's.

"Father, look," he said. "She's going home."

Far out over the stormy ocean, close to the waves,

riding the wind, the albatross was on her way.

If you enjoyed this book, you might also like:

978-1-4063-5559-8

978-1-4063-7919-8

978-1-4063-8293-8

978-1-4063-9133-6

Available from all good booksellers

www.walker.co.uk